SURF'S UP, GIZMO!

WRITTEN BY **SUZANNE KLINE**

ILLUSTRATED BY **JIM HUNT**

Gizmo says, "Let's surf to the back of the book to practice being calm, mindful, and balanced."

"Look for my colorful surfboards to lead the way. It is easy to *Just Surf IT* when you know how."

~Gizmo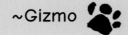

Dedication

This book is dedicated to Susan, Jim, Bonnie, Leah, and Colin for all their amazing insight, support, creative talents, and encouragement in making this book a reality. I am grateful to the devoted teachers in our schools who help children to become self-aware, resilient, compassionate, and mindful learners that make this world a fun place to be.

To Cosmo, my furry buddy who started it all. You are forever in my heart.

www.SurfsUpGizmo.com

Mom tucked Gizmo into his cozy bed and kissed him goodnight after his fun day at the beach. As he closed his eyes, Gizmo imagined he was still surfing and snorkeling with his friends Benny the Octopus and Molly the Dolphin.

Gizmo thought about the way the sunlight made everything sparkle underwater.

He had so many questions. Do sea creatures sleep? Do they swim while they sleep?

All this thinking made him tired.

Soon he was fast asleep, as happy as a clam at high tide!

Gizmo was dreaming about his swimming race with Molly the Dolphin when he suddenly woke up with a tummy ache.

"Uh oh!" he barked. "I don't feel well."

He shivered under the covers, hoping his tummy ache was just a bad dream. But it wasn't.

He barked for Mom.

Mom heard Gizmo's loud barking and hurried into his room. She pulled back his covers and saw that Gizmo's belly rolled like a wave and looked like a beach ball.

"Mom, my tummy hurts and feels really strange," Gizmo woofed.

"Oh my, Gizmo! Our tummies are not supposed to look or feel like that. We need to go to the hospital Emergency Room to have the doctor take a look at you."

Gizmo had never gone to the hospital before, and he didn't want to go.

Mom assured him, "Gizmo, I will be with you the whole time. I am sure the doctor will know just what to do."

They arrived at the Emergency Room where Alex, the nice attendant, greeted them with a big grin, "How about taking a spin in a wheelchair, Gizmo? I can tell you are a very brave dog."

4

Gizmo hopped on the wheelchair and laughed, "Let's go faster!"

He held on tight to the wheelchair, with his toes curled, at every fast turn in the hospital hallway.

Alex reminded Gizmo to stay within the hospital speed limit or he might get a ticket.

Gizmo rolled into an examination room filled with interesting equipment and lots of flashing lights.

Nurse Abby asked Gizmo to hop onto the bed and put on the colorful hospital gown decorated with cats, of all things!

"Uh oh...cats?" Gizmo whimpered, "I don't want to wear a gown. I just want to go home."

Nurse Abby smiled," I understand, Gizmo, but it will help the doctor look at your tummy. I bet a snuggly blanket will help you feel warm and cozy."

He whined, "Okay, Abby, I will wear it."

Gizmo was a little nervous, so he imagined himself doing his favorite thing—catching waves with his friends Benny the Octopus and Molly the Dolphin.

He closed his eyes, took slow deep breaths, and pictured himself as a surfer dog "hanging ten" on his surfboard. Gizmo turned his surfboard into the wave and felt powerful and brave carving through the mighty ocean.

He was starting to see the hospital experience as just another challenging wave.

Gizmo snuggled into the soft blanket that had fun ocean scenes. It felt warm and cuddly.

Abby told Gizmo that she had to take his temperature, and quick as a tail wag, she reported, "All is well, Gizmo."

Gizmo trusted Nurse Abby and gave her his paw so she could count his heartbeats.

Abby was a very kind nurse. She could tell that Gizmo was a little nervous and knew just what to do. "Hey, Gizmo, would you like to listen to your strong heartbeat with the stethoscope?"

Gizmo's ears perked right up when he heard his steady and powerful heartbeats.

Ba boom ♥♥♥♥

Ba boom ♥♥♥♥

Ba boom ♥♥♥♥

8

Gizmo let his mind float back to the beach, remembering to stay calm by practicing his deep breathing.

He thought about Benny having three hearts and wondered how anyone could check his blood pressure. The cuff felt like Benny giving him a big hug with all six of his arms and two legs.

Gizmo stayed relaxed, and the blood pressure check was over in a flash!

Doctor Cindy entered the room and gave Gizmo the best hug ever! With his tail wagging, Gizmo cuddled into her big hug.

"So, Gizmo, what is going on with your tummy?"

All Gizmo could report was that it hurt bad and sort of tickled, too.

"All right, buddy, let's take a look."

Doctor Cindy was surprised at the sight of Gizmo's belly that rolled with every breath. Just as she touched it, he let out a big burp of bright orange bubbles!

"Oh my, Gizmo, I'm happy you came to the hospital," said Doctor Cindy. "It looks like you will need to stay here a while so we can find out what is inside that tummy of yours."

BUUURRRRP!

With his sad puppy-dog eyes, Gizmo begged, "Please, Mom. Let's just go home."

Mom was very wise. "I have an idea, Gizmo; let's relax and breathe together. We can help each other stay calm while Doctor Cindy figures out why you have this tummy ache."

"Okay Mom, I'll try," replied Gizmo.

Alex brought Gizmo into a magical hospital room. He saw all the beautiful sea creatures swimming in the blue-green ocean.

Gizmo felt happy to be reminded of the beach he loved.

He wished he were there.

Gizmo loved his fun hospital bed.

"Yippie! This is the best bed ever!"
His head and feet moved up and
down at the push of a button. It
was so relaxing that he imagined
wearing his cool shades and
bobbing on the waves.

When Mom told Gizmo she was
going to stay in his room with
him, he gave her a big hug and a
sloppy lick on the cheek.

Alex took Gizmo to the x-ray department where Lea, the technician, greeted him with a big smile. She explained the machine would take a picture of the inside of his tummy.

"Gizmo, can you keep really still and hold your breath while I take the picture?"

"I can do it, Lea," he barked.

"Okay, Gizmo, then smile and say 'biscuit'!"

Lea's eyes widened with surprise at what she saw on the x-ray screen.

A clown fish blinked back at her!

"Hey, Gizmo, I think I know why your tummy feels funny and tickles!"

"How in the world did this clown fish get in there?"

"I'll tell Doctor Cindy right away. She will know what to do."

Gizmo watched the clown fish with
her cute face smiling back at him. He
remembered burping the bright orange bubbles.

"I know; I'm going to name you Bubbles,"
said Gizmo.

He felt better as he imagined meeting
her someday.

GULP!

Gizmo remembered gulping a lot of water while playing in the waves. Could he have accidentally slurped a fish?

As a dog, he did tend to swallow some pretty strange things.

All this thinking made him tired! He cuddled up in his cozy blanket as he slowly breathed—

in and out...

in and out.

Focusing on his breath always helped him.

Doctor Cindy entered the room and introduced the surgeon, Doctor Colin. The doctors shared the surprising news about the x-ray, along with the plan they had for an operation to help Gizmo and Bubbles feel better.

Mom held Gizmo's paw and asked the doctors lots of questions.

Mom knew it would be all right.

Gizmo snuggled into his blanket and focused on his breathing. It always helped him to relax— and make the scary thoughts disappear.

Mom hugged Gizmo and softly whispered in his ear, "Gizmo, everything will be all right."

"The operation is just like taking a restful nap. I promise that I will be right here when you wake up."

Soft music was playing when Gizmo arrived in the operating room.

The music had the familiar sounds of the ocean surf and dolphins in every note.

The music worked!

Gizmo felt calm and happy imagining himself as a deep sea diver, swimming and playing in the reefs with all his ocean buddies. He was soon fast asleep.

Gizmo dreamed about his
best friend Molly.

Molly swam beside Gizmo
and Bubbles, guiding them
with her powerful sonar. Her
dolphin clicks and whistles
helped everyone navigate
easily through the water.

She never left Gizmo's side.

While Gizmo slept, everyone in the operating room was busy. Nurses and doctors worked as a team to help Gizmo and Bubbles.

Nurse Abby held his paw and whispered, "Gizmo, you are doing just great."

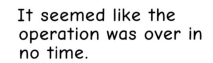

It seemed like the operation was over in no time.

Doctor Colin plopped the little clown fish into her cute fishbowl as everyone cheered.

He announced, "Everyone, meet Bubbles!"

Gizmo opened his eyes to see Mom's smiling face, just as she had promised him.

All at once, Gizmo noticed the fishbowl. "Wow, Bubbles! It's really you," he howled. "I feel better. How about you?"

"Yes, Gizmo, I feel lots better," she giggled. "Let's be friends!"

"Yay!" he barked. "Surf's up, Bubbles—let's go surfing!"

Mom smiled, "Okay, you two. First, a little more rest. "

WELCOME HoME BUBBLES!

Gizmo was happy to leave the hospital. He held on tightly to Bubbles' fishbowl while Mom drove to his favorite beach. It was a big surprise to see everyone cheering as he released Bubbles.

The dolphins celebrated by jumping, flipping, and spinning in the air.

Riding home, Mom reminded Gizmo to wear his mask and snorkel the next time he swims the surf.

"Don't worry, Mom. I will," said Gizmo.

His mind drifted, remembering his hospital adventure and how it connected him to his new friends, especially Bubbles. He thought about how you never know where life's crazy adventures will lead. Just like catching an awesome wave, sometimes you need to relax and enjoy the ride....

JUST SURF IT!

Let's Surf IT with Gizmo!

What does Gizmo do when life's waves are high and the surf gets rough? He shakes it off and reminds himself that everything will be okay.

He balances on his surfboard and he...

stretches his arms out wide, taking a deep breath in and letting a deep breath out through his mouth like a big sigh: "Ahhhhhhh!"

He closes his mouth and takes another slow, deep breath in—watching his tummy expand like a big beach ball...then he slowly lets it out—feeling his tummy fall flat.

He takes four more of these slow, deep breaths. When he slowly breathes in...and then slowly breathes out, making the Ahhhhhhh sound...
it begins to sound just like the waves of the ocean!

Now he is calm, relaxed, powerful, and ready to *Just Surf IT!*

Now you try it!

Like Gizmo says, "Feel balanced on your board and keep the wind behind your tail!"

Let go of whatever is bothering you or making you upset.

Breathe in and out and make those ocean sounds five times.

Feel the calm waves return with each relaxing breath.

Now, giggle and wiggle your fingers and toes and shake it off.

Gizmo says this will make you feel like he does when he's wagging his tail.

And smile, knowing you have people who LOVE YOU!